GRAPHIC NOVELS

STONE ARCH BOOKS
a capstone imprint

UP NEXT)))

on **Sports Illustrated KIDS**

:02 SPORTS ZONE SPECIAL REPORT

:04 FEATURE PRESENTATION:

AVALANCHE FREESTYLE

FOLLOWED BY:

:50 SPORTS ZONE
POSTGAME RECAP

:51 SPORTS ZONE
POSTGAME EXTRA

:52 SI KIDS INFO CENTER

N SHREDDERS FROM ALL OVER WILL MEET AT SILVER FALLS SKI R   SIK TICKER

TOP-RANKED TONY JAY IS EARLY FAVORITE TO WIN SILVER FALLS TOURNAMENT

TONY JAY

STATS:
AGE: 15
EVENT: FREESTYLE

BIO: Tony's father, Calvin Jay, is the owner o
Silver Falls Ski Resort. Calvin bought his so
the best gear that money can buy, and Tony'
skills are second to none. In fact, the onl
shredder who has a shot at taking down Tony i
Jack Hewlitt. There's just one problem — poo
Jack can't afford to enter the competitio
meaning that Tony will likely take home firs
place — and the fabled Aurora-X snowboard!

JACK HEWLITT

AGE: 15

EVENT: FREESTYLE

BIO: Jack is a gifted shredder despite having to use a shabby board and well-worn bindings. Although his equipment is nowhere near top-notch, his skills are second to none, and he'll give Tony Jay a run for his money if he can find a way to enter the tournament...

BLZ vs BKS
3·1
TGR vs ROR
33:32
EAG vs BAN
14:7
SPA vs WLD
4·3
BAN vs LIG
21-15
ROR vs LIG
4·3
BLZ vs BKS
3·1

DWAYNE KENT

AGE: 15

BIO: Dwayne is one of Tony Jay's many friends. Like Janice and Kevin, Dwayne is almost always hanging out at the Jay family's mansion.

DWAYNE

CALVIN JAY

AGE: 43

BIO: Tony's father is a wealthy businessman who made a fortune in the music business. Now, he owns and runs the Silver Falls Ski Resort.

CALVIN

MARC HEWLITT

AGE: 47

BIO: Jack's father is a maintenance worker at Silver Falls Ski Resort. He does not make much money, but he loves his job — and his son.

MARC

PRESENTS

A PRODUCTION OF

STONE ARCH BOOKS
a capstone imprint

written by Scott Ciencin

Illustrated by Aburtov

Inked by Andres Esparza

Colored by Fares Maese

designed and directed by Bob Lentz
edited by Sean Tulien
creative direction by Heather Kindseth
editorial direction by Michael Dahl

Summary: Rich kid Tony Jay is a sure bet to win the Silver Falls snowboarding tournament, but his biggest competition, Jack Hewlitt, can't afford to enter. Tony may be spoiled, but he knows that victory means nothing if you don't beat the best. So, he agrees to hold a one-on-one freestyle contest with Jack atop the Silver Falls Mountains. But just when things start to heat up, a massive avalanche threatens to put both boys on ice, turning their friendly competition into a race for their lives.

Sports Illustrated KIDS *Avalanche Freestyle* is published by Stone Arch Books,
710 Roe Crest Drive, North Mankato, Minnesota 56003.
www.capstonepub.com

Cataloging-in-Publication Data is available at the Library of Congress website.

ISBN: 978-1-4342-2009-7 (library binding)
ISBN: 978-1-4342-2783-6 (paperback)
ISBN: 978-1-4342-4938-8 (e-book)

Printed in the United States of America.
032019   000072

LL GO TO THE WINNER OF HIS SNOWBOARDING TOURNAMENT   SIK TICKER

This is the Silver Falls Ski Resort. My dad owns it.

A week from now, the resort will host the second annual Silver Falls Snowboarding Competition at our superpipe.

Up for grabs is the Aurora-X, the best board on the market — and I plan on taking first place.

Who am I? My name is Tony Jay . . .

Meanwhile...

There you are, troublemaker. What are you up to?

Trouble.

That's my boy.

Make yourself useful and carry the first-aid kit.

THUNK!

Hey, what if someone notices that the board's gone?

Don't worry about it . . .

". . . They'll find Jack's lift pass right where I left it."

JACK HEWLITT

21

"You get points for coming in first ..."

FWOOSHH

"... But you also get points for tricks."

"To make things fair, we'll score each other."

NO
OARDING

BITTER RIVALS BECOME FAST FRIENDS AFTER OUTRUNNING AVALANCHE TOGETHER

BY THE NUMBERS

FREESTYLE EVENT FINAL SCORES:

ONY JAY: 9.6
ACK HEWLITT: 9.6
Y TAGGART: 9.7

STORY: An avalanche interrupted a freestyle due between Jack Hewlitt and Tony Jay this weekend. The two teens were competing for the Aurora-X under the assumption that Tony Jay would later win it in the tournament. The unexpected event didn't faze the two teens — they simply shredded their way down the mountain with the deadly maelstrom of snow and ice nipping at their bindings.

Sports ustrated KIDS

UP NEXT: SI KIDS INFO CENTER

SZ **POSTGAME EXTRA**

WHERE **YOU** ANALYZE THE GAME!

BLZ vs BNS
3-1
TGR vs ROR
33-32
EAG vs BAN
14-7
SPA vs WLD
4-3
BAN vs ROR
21-15
ROR vs LIG
4-3
BLZ vs BNS
3-1

Snowboarding fans got a real treat today when Tony Jay faced off against Jack Hewlitt in the Silver Falls Freestyle Tournament. Let's go into the stands and ask some fans for their opinions on the day's events...

DISCUSSION QUESTION 1

Tony Jay and Jack Hewlitt are total opposites in some ways. Do you think people who are very different can become good friends? Why or why not?

DISCUSSION QUESTION 2

Who do you like better — Tony Jay or Jack Hewlitt? What kinds of things do you like, and dislike, about each teen? Discuss your answers.

WRITING PROMPT 1

Imagine that you've won a snowboarding tournament, and your reward is a custom board! Name your new board, and write a few paragraphs about it. Then, draw a picture of your personalized reward.

WRITING PROMPT 2

Both Tony and Jack act like heroes at certain points in this book. Have you ever seen or done something heroic? What happened? Write about it.

(AIR)—if you grab air, you perform a jump of some sort

(AV-uh-lanch)—a large mass of snow, ice, and earth that suddenly moves down the side of a mountain

(BINDE-ingz)—the part of a snowboard that you connect boots to

(free-STILE)—a style of skiing or snowboarding focused on doing tricks

(HAF-pipe)—a U-shaped trench with smooth walls that is used by snowboarders for aerial tricks

(SHRED-ur)—a snowboarder, particularly a talented one

(SPON-sur)—to give money and support to someone who is competing in a contest of some kind

(SOO-pur-pipe)—a larger version of a regular halfpipe. The walls in a superpipe can measure as high as 20 feet.

EATORS

SCOTT CIENCIN › Author

Scott Ciencin is a *New York Times* bestselling author of children's and adult fiction. He has written comic books, trading cards, video games, television shows, as well as many non-fiction projects. He lives in Sarasota, Florida with his beloved wife, Denise, and his best buddy, Bear, a golden retriever. He loves writing books for Stone Arch, and is working hard on many more that are still to come.

ABURTOV › Illustrator

Aburtov is a graphic designer and illustrator who has worked in the comic book industry for more than 11 years. In that time, Aburtov has colored popular characters like Wolverine, Iron Man, Punisher, and Blade. He recently created his own studio called Graphikslava. Aburtov lives with his beloved wife in Monterrey, Mexico, where he enjoys spending time with family and friends.

ANDRES ESPARZA › Inker

Andres Esparza has been a graphic designer, colorist, and illustrator for many different companies and agencies. Andres now works as a full-time artist for Graphikslava studio in Monterrey, Mexico. In his spare time, Andres loves to play basketball, hang out with family and friends, and listen to good music.

FARES MAESE › Colorist

Fares Maese is a graphic designer and illustrator. He has worked as a colorist for Marvel Comics, and as a concept artist for the card and role-playing games Pathfinder and Warhammer. Fares loves spending time playing video games with his Graphikslava comrades, and he's an awesome drum player.

)) LOVE THIS QUICK COMIC? READ THE WHOLE STORY IN
SKATEBOARD BREAKDOWN – ONLY FROM STONE ARCH BOOKS

STONE ARCH BOOKS

a capstone imprint